Kitty
the Tiger
Fairy

Special thanks to Narinder Dhami

No part of this work may be reproduced, stored in a retrieval system, or transmitted in any form or by any means, electronic, mechanical, photocopying, recording, or otherwise, without written permission of the publisher. For information regarding permission, write to Rainbow Magic Limited c/o HIT Entertainment, 830 South Greenville Avenue, Allen, TX 75002-3320.

ISBN 978-0-545-70846-3

All rights reserved. Published by Scholastic Inc., 557 Broadway, New York, NY 10012, by arrangement with Rainbow Magic Limited.

SCHOLASTIC and associated logos are trademarks and/or registered trademarks of Scholastic Inc. RAINBOW MAGIC is a trademark of Rainbow Magic Limited. Reg. U.S. Patent & Trademark Office and other countries. HIT and the HIT logo are trademarks of HIT Entertainment Limited.

12 11 10 9 8 7 6 5 4 3 2 1   15 16 17 18 19/0

Printed in the U.S.A.   40

First Scholastic printing, January 2015

Kitty
the Tiger
Fairy

by Daisy Meadows

SCHOLASTIC INC.

The Fairyland Palace

Meadow

Stream

Beehive

Arctic Tundra

Eucalyptus Forest

Tropical Waterfall

Wild Woods
Nature
Reserve

Watering Hole

Pagoda

Jack Frost's
Ice Castle

To Jack Frost's Zoo

Desert Oasis

I love animals—yes, I do,
I want my very own private zoo!
I'll capture all the animals one by one,
With fairy magic to help me get it done!

A koala, a tiger, an Arctic fox,
I'll keep them in cages with giant locks.
Every kind of animal will be there,
A panda, a meerkat, a honey bear.
The animals will be my property,
I'll be master of my own menagerie!

Contents

Return to Wild Woods

"I can't wait to find out what we'll be doing today!" Rachel Walker exclaimed eagerly as she followed her best friend, Kirsty Tate, through Wild Woods Nature Reserve. "I hope we see lots of different animals."

It was summer vacation, and the girls' parents had arranged for them to spend a week as junior rangers at Kirsty's local

nature reserve. The reserve was a haven for all kinds of animals like hares, otters, and red squirrels.

"We'll have lots of cool pictures to remind us of our time here at Wild Woods," Kirsty remarked as the girls wound their way through the trees, carrying their backpacks. She stopped to take a picture of a red-and-blue butterfly drinking nectar from a cluster of wildflowers. She showed the photo to Rachel.

"It's beautiful," Rachel said with admiration as Kirsty slipped the camera into her backpack. "Look, Kirsty, there's

Becky with the other junior rangers." She pointed to the clearing ahead of them where a group of girls and boys were gathered around the head of the nature reserve. "I bet she has some interesting jobs for us!"

Becky was chatting with a couple of the junior rangers. She spotted the girls and waved to them.

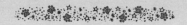

"Everyone's here now, so good morning to you all," Becky announced with a huge smile. "I'm thrilled you're back for more important wildlife work here at Wild Woods Nature Reserve! Did you have a good time yesterday?"

"YES!" everyone shouted, full of excitement.

"Well, we have a very busy day ahead of us," she informed them. "I have a special job for you down at the stream. You can start off by getting yourselves dressed in *these*!" Becky pointed to a bunch of tall rubber boots piled on the grass beside her. Rachel and Kirsty lined

up with the other junior rangers to grab
a pair, and then they pulled on the
rubber boots. The boots were so tall,
they covered their legs all the way up to
their thighs.

"I feel like Puss-in-
Boots!" Kirsty
said to Rachel
with a grin.

Becky
grabbed a
rake that
was leaning
against a
nearby tree
and a net
lying on the
grass. "Follow me, everyone," she called,
walking off through the woods.

"I wonder why we're going to the stream," Rachel remarked as everyone followed Becky. "I hope we'll be able to do the special job, whatever it is."

"If we finish it, we might get another badge," Kirsty said hopefully. Becky had given the girls badges with a picture of a tree on them after they'd successfully planted some young saplings the day before. Rachel and Kirsty had proudly

pinned the badges to their backpacks. "And maybe"—Kirsty lowered her voice so that no one else could hear—"our fairy friends will need our help again today, too!"

When the girls had arrived at the nature reserve yesterday, they'd been thrilled to see their friend Bertram, a frog footman from Fairyland. Bertram was visiting relatives who lived in a pond in Wild Woods, and he'd offered to take the girls to the Fairyland Nature Reserve. Of course, Rachel and Kirsty had agreed immediately. At the Fairyland Reserve, their old friend Fluffy the squirrel was their guide, and they'd seen lots of fascinating animals, like penguins in the ice and snow, and monkeys swinging through the jungle.

The girls had also met the seven Baby Animal Rescue Fairies whose job it was to look after the Fairyland Nature Reserve and to protect wildlife everywhere, in both the fairy and human worlds.

Rachel and Kirsty had been having a wonderful time with their fairy friends until Jack Frost turned up and ruined everything! Jack Frost had declared that he liked animals so much, he was going to collect one of each kind for his private zoo. Then, with a magic ice bolt, he stole the Baby Animal Rescue Fairies' charms—the tiny, furry animal key chains that helped them care for wildlife. Jack Frost then gave the key chains to his goblins, and ordered them to hurry away

to the human world and bring him some animals for his zoo!

"We need to keep an eye out for goblins as well as wildlife," Rachel whispered. The girls had promised to help the Baby Animal Rescue Fairies retrieve their magic key chains, and also protect the animals that selfish Jack Frost wanted to capture for his private zoo. The fairies had been very grateful. All seven of them had waved their wands together, and their combined magic had granted Rachel and Kirsty the power to talk to animals.

"It was so mean of the goblins to kidnap Pan Pan the baby panda yesterday," Kirsty recalled as Becky led them deeper into the woods. "But at least we were

able to rescue him and take him back to his mother. Wasn't it amazing talking to a real-live panda, Rachel?"

"Awesome!" Rachel agreed. "Pan Pan was so cute!" She glanced around. "I can hear water trickling, Kirsty. We must be close to the stream."

Kirsty took her camera out and snapped a few pictures. The forest was beautiful in the early morning light.

Becky led the junior rangers past a clump of oak trees toward the stream. But what the girls saw ahead of them made them come to an abrupt stop and gasp in horror.

"Oh, no!" Kirsty cried. "What happened to the stream?"

Kitty Comes for Help

Everyone could see that the little stream was a complete mess. In one place, there was an ugly pile of dead leaves, twigs, and overgrown reeds that had created a dam, blocking the flow of water. When the water reached the dam, it had nowhere to go, so the stream was overflowing its banks. This made the ground damp and soggy. But below the dam there was hardly even a trickle of water, and the girls could see the dry bed of the stream.

"This is really bad for the wildlife in and around the stream," Becky explained, frowning. "We *have* to get the water flowing freely again." She turned to Rachel and Kirsty. "I'd like you two to do this job, please."

"Okay," the girls agreed eagerly. Kirsty put her camera away.

"One of you can clear away the mess," Becky went on. She began pulling at the dam with the rake, loosening some twigs and leaves. "Then the other can use the net to scoop the stuff out of the water." Becky handed the rake to Kirsty and showed Rachel how to drag the net across the surface of the water, collecting all the leaves and twigs. "Can you do that?"

The girls nodded.

"Excellent!" Becky flashed them a smile. "I'll come back when I've shown the others their jobs farther up the stream. Just pile up all the stuff you scoop out on the bank, girls. We can make compost with it. We try to be as green as we can here at Wild Woods!"

"No problem," Rachel called as Becky and the other junior rangers left.

The girls got to work. Kirsty used the rake to break up the dam and Rachel tried to catch every piece of leaf and twig in her net so she could remove it from the water. It was hard work, but they were determined to get the stream flowing freely again.

Suddenly, the flapping of wings overhead made both girls look up. Rachel gasped as she saw a large bird with gray, white, and black feathers flying toward them.

"Oh, it's a heron!" Rachel exclaimed.

"Isn't she beautiful?" Kirsty said with a sigh, her eyes wide.

"Thank you for cleaning up the stream," the heron called to them in a

high, sweet voice. "I'm looking forward
to fishing downstream once the water is
flowing again."

"You're welcome," Kirsty called. She
and Rachel waved as the heron flew off
over the treetops.

"Being able to talk to animals is so
much fun!" Rachel said happily as they
got back to work.

A few moments later, Rachel heard
a rustling among the
reeds. She glanced
over and saw three
pairs of bright, dark
eyes watching her.
Rachel smiled when
she realized that it was
a mother otter with her two babies, and
she pointed them out to Kirsty.

"Hello, there," Kirsty said to the otters. "Can we help you?"

"I was hoping to teach my babies to swim," the mother otter explained, twitching her whiskers. "But the stream is too deep on one side of this dam and too shallow on the other."

"We're clearing away the dam," Kirsty told her. "Why don't you come back a little later?"

"Good idea," the mother otter agreed.
"Thank you!" And the three otters
scampered away.

The girls continued pulling the dam
apart. More water was beginning to
trickle through here and there, which
encouraged them to keep working.

"See that big log?" Rachel punted,
pointing it out to Kirsty. "I think that's
keeping a lot of water from getting
through. Let's try to pull it out."

Kirsty pulled at the log with her rake,
but it didn't budge, even though she put
all her weight into it. Rachel threw the
net down and went to help her, but even
between them, they couldn't move the
log at all. It was stuck fast. Both girls
tried and tried, but they were puffing
and panting, now out of breath.

"Let's take a break." Kirsty gasped.

There was nowhere to sit down except on the wet ground, so the girls leaned against a nearby tree and rested for a few moments.

"I think we need an energy boost!" Rachel said with a grin. "I packed some cereal bars."

Rachel opened her backpack and took out her tiger-print lunch box. As she took the lid off, the girls were surprised to see a magic golden glow coming from inside. Then they saw a little fairy flutter out of the lunch box and hover, smiling, in the air before them.

"Kitty the Tiger Fairy!" Kirsty exclaimed.

Tiger Talk

"Hi, girls!" Kitty said. She was dressed in a sleeveless top with diagonal stripes, rolled-up jeans, and ankle boots. She also wore a headband with tiger ears on top of her blond curls. "I'm sure you can guess why I'm here."

"Jack Frost's goblins are trying to catch more animals?" Rachel guessed.

Kitty nodded. "Right now those mischievous goblins are chasing three tiger cubs, hoping to capture one for Jack Frost's zoo," she replied, frowning anxiously. "And I can't protect the cubs with my magic because the goblins have my magic key chain."

"Can we help?" Kirsty offered eagerly.

Kitty smiled. "Thank you, girls," she replied. "Let's go and stop those dreadful goblins. They can't get away with kidnapping my beautiful tigers!"

Kitty shook her wand, conjuring up a cloud of glittering fairy dust. The girls were whisked gently away and, in the blink of an eye, Rachel and Kirsty found themselves thousands of miles from the nature reserve. They landed in a beautiful, faraway jungle where they

could feel the heat of the red-gold sun
overhead. They were standing on a rock
jutting out over a river that flowed down
from a beautiful, high waterfall. The
banks of the river were lined with tall
trees and tropical flowers.

"I wonder what happened to my poor little tiger cubs?" Kitty said anxiously.

Before Rachel or Kirsty could say anything, they heard a loud roar coming from among the trees.

"GO AWAY!"

"Who's that?" Rachel asked cautiously. She and Kirsty turned to look. Suddenly the girls saw two tiger cubs slip out from behind a tree and prowl toward them. They looked ready to pounce!

Immediately, Kitty swooped down lower. "Don't worry, little ones," she called to the tiger cubs. "These are my friends. You're very safe."

The tiger cubs stopped, looking uncertainly at the girls.

"They're not green like the others!" the biggest cub growled.

"We're not green because we're girls, not goblins," Rachel explained gently.

"And we want to help you, not hurt you," Kirsty added.

The tiger cubs looked much happier.

"Let me introduce you," Kitty said with a smile. "Cubs, these are my friends Rachel and Kirsty. Girls, this is Stripes"—she pointed her wand at the biggest cub—"and this is Tig, his brother."

"Pleased to meet you!" Stripes and Tig declared in their cute, growly little cub voices.

"But, boys, where's your sister, Sheba?" Kitty went on, looking worried. "You three are *always* together."

"We got separated when the little green boys started chasing us," Stripes replied, his voice full of concern.

"We've been looking for Sheba for a while," Tig explained. "We followed her scent to the river, but it stops here."

"Sheba must have managed to get

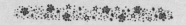

across to the other side of the river," Kitty guessed.

"Tig and I were going to swim over and look for her," said Stripes, "but then we hid in the trees because we thought you were coming to catch us!"

"We'll help you search for Sheba," Rachel offered.

"Thank you," Tig said gratefully. "We'd offer you a ride on our backs if you were a little bit smaller."

"Well, that's one problem easily solved!" Kitty laughed. With a flick of her wand, she scattered magic sparkles around the girls, turning them both into fairies.

Full of excitement, Rachel and Kirsty
flew over to the tiger cubs. Kirsty floated
down onto Stripes's
back, and Rachel
landed on Tig.
*The cub's fur
is as thick, soft,
and warm as a
blanket,* Rachel
thought as she
stroked Tig's
head.

With the girls clinging onto their furry
necks, the two cubs bounded into the
river and began to swim. Kitty flew just
above them, keeping an eye on what was
going on beneath her. The cubs were
racing against each other, seeing who
could swim the fastest. Tig playfully

splashed Stripes with his little paw, and
Rachel and Kirsty burst out laughing.

"Hey, stop that!" Stripes growled. He
scooped up some water in his paw and
tossed it at his brother. A few drops flew
upward and splashed Kitty's clothes as
she zoomed along above them.

"Sorry, Kitty!" Stripes called.

"Just keep swimming!" Kitty told him with a smile.

When the tiger cubs reached the other side of the river, they waded out of the water onto the bank. Rachel and Kirsty fluttered off their backs, and the cubs shook themselves vigorously to dry their wet fur. Then the two of them were off, noses to the ground, trying to pick up their sister's scent.

"Sheba's been here!" Tig announced, his tail twitching with excitement. "We

can smell her." He and Stripes began sniffing their way along the trail Sheba had left. Kitty, Rachel, and Kirsty flew after them, following the tiger cubs along the riverbank toward the waterfall.

"I can't see Sheba anywhere," Kitty murmured.

"Maybe she's hiding if she's frightened of the goblins," Rachel suggested.

Suddenly, Stripes and Tig stopped, perking up their ears.

"We can hear something!" Stripes told Kitty and the girls.

Kitty beckoned to Rachel and Kirsty. Silently, the three of them flew ahead of the cubs and they heard the faint sound of rough, gruff voices.

"It sounds like goblins!" Kirsty whispered.

Tree Goblins!

Kitty, Rachel, and Kirsty wound their way through the lush green jungle. They followed the sound of the voices. After a few moments, Rachel spotted three goblins climbing up the trunk of a tree ahead of them.

"There they are!" Rachel murmured, pointing them out to Kitty and Kirsty.

"Let's fly higher up the same tree," Kitty suggested. "Then we can listen to what they're saying. We should be able to find out where Sheba is, as well as my key chain!"

Keeping high in the air so that the goblins wouldn't spot them, Kitty led the way over to the tree. She floated down onto one of the higher branches, and Rachel and Kirsty landed next to her.

Kirsty peered through the leaves. She could see the three goblins below them. They weren't very good climbers, and they were huffing and puffing as they tried to move up from branch to branch.

"This is all your fault!" the goblin who was highest up the tree screeched at the one just below him. "You lost the fairy's magic tiger key chain!"

"Lost!" Kitty repeated under her breath, looking disappointed.

"It wasn't *my* fault," the second goblin whined. "Not really."

The third goblin was even lower down the tree and was struggling to swing himself up to the next branch. He made a giant, desperate lunge and ended up hanging upside down from the branch by his feet, like a bat.

Kitty and the girls tried hard not to laugh at him.

"I need help!" the goblin shrieked.

The first and second goblins ignored him and kept arguing.

"*You* were carrying the fairy's magic key chain," the first goblin shouted accusingly. "And now you don't have it—so it *must* be your fault!"

The second goblin looked sheepish. "I wasn't expecting those tiger cubs to be so scary," he mumbled. "And anyway, the magic key chain isn't *really* lost—we know where it is. The smallest tiger cub has it."

Kitty glanced excitedly at the girls. "That's Sheba!" she whispered.

Suddenly, there was a rustling in the undergrowth down below. The next moment, Stripes and Tig burst out and

raced toward the tree, growling fiercely.
The girls could understand what the cubs
were roaring. They were saying: *Where's
our sister?*

The goblins were terrified. Two of
them hauled the third
up to join
them, and
they all sat
shivering
and
shaking on
the branch
below Kitty
and the girls.
"I have an
idea how to find
Sheba *and* Kitty's magic key chain!"
Rachel whispered, her face lighting up.

Quickly, she explained her plan to Kitty and Kirsty, then the two girls flew down to the goblins.

"Oh, no!" shouted the first goblin. "Pesky fairies *and* scary tiger cubs!"

"Make them go away!" the second goblin yelled at the girls, pointing down at Stripes and Tig, who were growling loudly.

"We can understand tiger talk," Rachel said. "They're asking you where their sister is."

The three goblins glanced at each other. "We're not telling you!" the third goblin snapped rudely. Then he wobbled a little on the branch and shrieked with fright. "Tell them! Tell them!" he shouted at the others. "Otherwise we'll be stuck here forever *or* we'll fall out of the tree and the tigers will get us!"

"We saw her going up to the top of the big waterfall," the first goblin mumbled grumpily.

"But then we lost sight of her," the second goblin added.

Kitty, who had been listening above them, quickly swooped down to Stripes and Tig.

"The goblins don't have Sheba," she told the cubs. "She's somewhere near the top of the waterfall. Let them go."

Obediently, the tiger cubs stopped growling and sat down on the grass.

In the meantime, the three silly goblins hurried down the tree as fast as they could and ran off without a backward glance.

"Meet you at the top of the waterfall!" Stripes shouted to Kitty and the girls. "Come on, Tig!" The cubs ran toward the cliff as fast as they could in a blur of orange and black.

Kitty, Rachel, and Kirsty flew to the river and followed it to the pool at the

bottom of the waterfall. Then they
fluttered upward, enjoying the cool, fresh
air and the sight of the clear, sparkling
water tumbling down over the cliff. Kirsty
luughed as she flew a little too close and
droplets of water landed on her face.

"Isn't it beautiful?" She sighed.

"Gorgeous," Rachel agreed, turning

to look at the view of the river winding
along below them.

Kirsty glanced up and saw Stripes and
Tig waiting for them on top of the cliff.

But all of a sudden she saw another flash of orange and black *behind* the cascading waterfall.

"Is that you, Sheba?" Kirsty called. She squinted, trying to see farther, but the orange-and-black creature had disappeared.

Sheba's Splashing

Kirsty turned to Rachel and Kitty. "I think I just saw Sheba the tiger cub behind the waterfall!" she told them breathlessly.

"Let's go and see," Kitty said immediately. "I'm afraid we'll get pretty wet, though." She linked hands with Rachel and Kirsty. "Get ready, girls!"

Kirsty took a deep breath. They were about to get very, very wet. She just hoped it *was* Sheba that she'd seen!

Swiftly, the three friends zoomed around the falling sheet of water and landed on a ledge behind it. Now they were right in front of the cliff face.

"Look, there's a little cave over there," Rachel said, smoothing back her wet hair. "I wonder if Sheba's inside."

They peered into the cave. To Kirsty's delight, she saw a little tiger cub rolling around on the ground. She was playing with a tiger key chain, throwing it into the air and catching it between her paws. Kirsty could see the key chain was surrounded by a faint, golden glow that lit up the dark cave.

"My magic key chain!" Kitty said excitedly. "Hello, Sheba. You can come out of the cave now. The goblins are gone."

"Don't want to!" Sheba's growl was sassy, her golden eyes full of mischief. "I'm having too much fun!"

"Animals love our special key chains," Kitty reminded the girls, as Sheba continued batting the furry tiger around. "She won't give it up easily! But if we can find something else Sheba likes, then she might forget about my key chain."

"I'll see what I've got," said Rachel, searching in her pocket.

"Wait, remember how much Stripes and Tig enjoyed playing around in the water?" Kirsty said slowly. "Maybe Sheba would come out if she thought she was missing a whole lot of fun?"

"That's a great idea," Kitty agreed.

Kirsty peeked into the cave again. "It's time for a little tiger to splash around in

the river!" she said. "Come on, Sheba, you don't want to miss all the fun."

Sheba's eyes lit up. "Hooray!" she cried in her growly voice, dropping Kitty's tiger on the ground. She batted it across the cave to Kirsty with her paw. Then she ran out and jumped straight through the waterfall

into the pool not far
below them.

"Thank
goodness!"
Kitty
murmured
gratefully
as she rushed
over to retrieve
her magic charm. The
instant she touched it, the key chain
shrank down to its Fairyland size and
Kitty clipped it firmly to a belt loop on
her jeans.

As Kitty and the girls flew around the
waterfall once more, they could hear
splashing and yelps of delight below
them. Stripes and Tig had spotted Sheba
in the pool and rushed down from the

cliff to join her. The three cubs were
having a water fight!

Suddenly, Rachel saw the three goblins
rush out from the trees. "Be careful,
cubs!" she yelled. "Here come the
goblins again!"

"We need a tiger for Jack Frost's zoo!"
the first goblin shouted. "Grab them!"

"GO AWAY!" Stripes, Tig, and Sheba
roared in unison. The three goblins
shrieked in terror and huddled together

on the riverbank, their teeth chattering
with fright.

"You can't just take any animals you
want, no matter what Jack Frost says,"
Kitty said sternly as she, Rachel, and
Kirsty swooped down toward the goblins.

"You can't just collect animals like toys
or books, you know!" Rachel added.

Then Kirsty gasped in surprise. She'd
just spotted a large, fully grown tiger

standing on the rock jutting out over the river.

"There is an enormous tiger over on that rock!" Kirsty exclaimed nervously. "It looks really fierce . . ."

Going with the Flow

This was too much for the goblins. They fled immediately, falling over their own big feet to get away as fast as they could.

"It's the cubs' mother," Kitty explained. "Come and say hello." She led the girls over to the tiger. "These are my friends Rachel and Kirsty," Kitty told her.

"Hello, girls," the mother tiger said in a gentle voice. "Thank you for finding my cubs. I was extremely worried about them."

"Mother! Mother!" the cubs roared in chorus. They began paddling across the pool toward her.

"And thank you, Rachel and Kirsty, for finding my magic tiger key chain." Kitty patted the key chain attached to her jeans. "I'll be off to Fairyland now to tell them the good news!"

An idea popped into Kirsty's head.

"Before you go, Kitty, could you help us out at Wild Woods?" she asked.

"Of course!" Kitty said instantly.

They all called good-bye to the mother tiger, Stripes, Tig, and Sheba. Then Kitty's magic restored the girls to their normal size and whirled them off to Wild Woods Nature Reserve. Just a few seconds later, the three of them were back at the stream.

"We can't move that log," Kirsty explained, pointing it out to Kitty. "Can you help?"

"I certainly can," Kitty agreed, smiling. She tapped the log with her wand, showering it with fairy dust. The log immediately rose up out of the water, floated through the air, and came to rest on the bank of the stream.

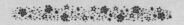

"Thank you, Kitty," Kirsty said happily. "Look, Rachel, the water's starting to flow again!"

The girls cheered as the water splashed through the gap left by the big, heavy log and began to fill up the dry bed of the stream.

"And now I really must go." Kitty smiled. "Good-bye, girls. I know I can count on you to help protect wildlife *everywhere* from Jack Frost and his

goblins!" She vanished in a puff of glittery fairy dust.

Then the girls heard the sound of beating wings overhead and the heron swooped down to land on the bank next to them.

"The water's flowing again!" the heron said excitedly. "Now I can fish downstream whenever I want." Rachel nudged Kirsty. "And here come the three otters!" she said.

The mother otter was leading her two babies to the edge of the water. "Hello, girls," she called to Rachel and Kirsty.

Then she turned to her babies. "Just do
what I do," she told them, and slipped
into the water. Her babies followed,
looking a little nervous.

"You're doing really well!" Kirsty
called, and she and Rachel applauded
as the baby otters paddled hesitantly
across the stream.

Suddenly, the girls heard the sound
of footsteps, and they saw Becky
approaching through the trees. The

heron flew away, and the otters swam
into a clump of reeds to hide.

"How are things going, girls?" Becky
asked. "You got the stream flowing
again—that's wonderful!" Then she
noticed the log on the bank. "How on
earth did you manage to move that?
Nice work! It'll be a perfect bench for
visitors."

Rachel and Kirsty grinned at each other.

"I think you both deserve a second badge," Becky added, handing one to Rachel and another to Kirsty. "As you can see, these badges have a picture of the stream on them."

The girls were thrilled.

"And I have another tricky task for you tomorrow," Becky went on, her eyes twinkling. "Do you think you'll be able to do it?"

"We hope so!" Rachel replied with a grin.

"A tricky task?" Kirsty whispered as Becky went off to check on the other junior rangers. "It *can't* be trickier than helping the Baby Animal Rescue Fairies protect wildlife from Jack Frost!"

"True," Rachel whispered back. "We'd better be ready for anything!"

Rachel and Kirsty found Mae and
Kitty's missing magic key chains.
Now it's time for them to help

Mara
the Meerkat Fairy!

Join their next adventure in this special
sneak peek . . .

A Very Tricky Task

"So, all we know about today's job is
that it's going to be especially tricky!"
Kirsty Tate remarked to her best friend,
Rachel Walker, as they made their way
along a path through the woods.

The two girls had volunteered to spend
a week of summer vacation working as
junior rangers at Wild Woods Nature
Reserve. "What do you think we'll be
doing, Rachel?"

"I don't know, but I'm looking forward to finding out when we meet Becky in the meadow!" Rachel replied with a grin. Becky was the head of the nature reserve. "I hope it's something we can do really well—and then we *might* earn another badge."

"I *love* getting badges," Kirsty said happily. She swung her backpack off her shoulders so she could proudly sneak a peek at the badges pinned to the pockets. This was the girls' third day at Wild Woods, and they'd already earned two badges because they'd successfully completed their tasks on the previous two days.

The girls heard a rustling noise in the undergrowth, and a little red squirrel scampered out of the bushes. He stopped in front of Rachel and Kirsty and gave them a mischievous glance.

"I heard what you were saying," the squirrel told them breathlessly. "And, you're right: You'll have a very difficult job to do today!" Then, giggling, he bounded away.

"Good luck!" chirped a voice from above. The girls looked up and saw a pair of goldfinches sitting on a branch side by side. "Like the squirrel said, you've got a very tricky task today."

"Very tricky!" the other goldfinch agreed. Then the two birds soared up into the blue sky.

"It's such amazing fun being able to talk to animals!" Rachel exclaimed. "We couldn't do it without the Baby Animal Rescue Fairies' magic."

Kirsty nodded. "I just wish we hadn't been given this magic for such a serious reason." She sighed. "We need the power to talk to animals so we can save wildlife everywhere from scary Jack Frost and his goblins!"

RAINBOW magic™

Which Magical Fairies Have You Met?

- ☐ The Rainbow Fairies
- ☐ The Weather Fairies
- ☐ The Jewel Fairies
- ☐ The Pet Fairies
- ☐ The Dance Fairies
- ☐ The Music Fairies
- ☐ The Sports Fairies
- ☐ The Party Fairies
- ☐ The Ocean Fairies
- ☐ The Night Fairies
- ☐ The Magical Animal Fairies
- ☐ The Princess Fairies
- ☐ The Superstar Fairies
- ☐ The Fashion Fairies
- ☐ The Sugar & Spice Fairies
- ☐ The Earth Fairies
- ☐ The Magical Crafts Fairies

■SCHOLASTIC

Find all of your favorite fairy friends at
scholastic.com/rainbowmagic

HIT entertainment

RMFAIRY11

SPECIAL EDITION

Which Magical Fairies Have You Met?

3 stories in each one!

- ☐ Joy the Summer Vacation Fairy
- ☐ Holly the Christmas Fairy
- ☐ Kylie the Carnival Fairy
- ☐ Stella the Star Fairy
- ☐ Shannon the Ocean Fairy
- ☐ Trixie the Halloween Fairy
- ☐ Gabriella the Snow Kingdom Fairy
- ☐ Juliet the Valentine Fairy
- ☐ Mia the Bridesmaid Fairy
- ☐ Flora the Dress-Up Fairy
- ☐ Paige the Christmas Play Fairy
- ☐ Emma the Easter Fairy
- ☐ Cara the Camp Fairy
- ☐ Destiny the Rock Star Fairy
- ☐ Belle the Birthday Fairy
- ☐ Olympia the Games Fairy
- ☐ Selena the Sleepover Fairy
- ☐ Cheryl the Christmas Tree Fairy
- ☐ Florence the Friendship Fairy
- ☐ Lindsay the Luck Fairy
- ☐ Brianna the Tooth Fairy
- ☐ Autumn the Falling Leaves Fairy
- ☐ Keira the Movie Star Fairy
- ☐ Addison the April Fool's Day Fairy
- ☐ Bailey the Babysitter Fairy
- ☐ Natalie the Christmas Stocking Fairy
- ☐ Lila and Myla the Twins Fairies

■SCHOLASTIC

Find all of your favorite fairy friends at
scholastic.com/rainbowmagic

HIT entertainment

RMSPECIAL14